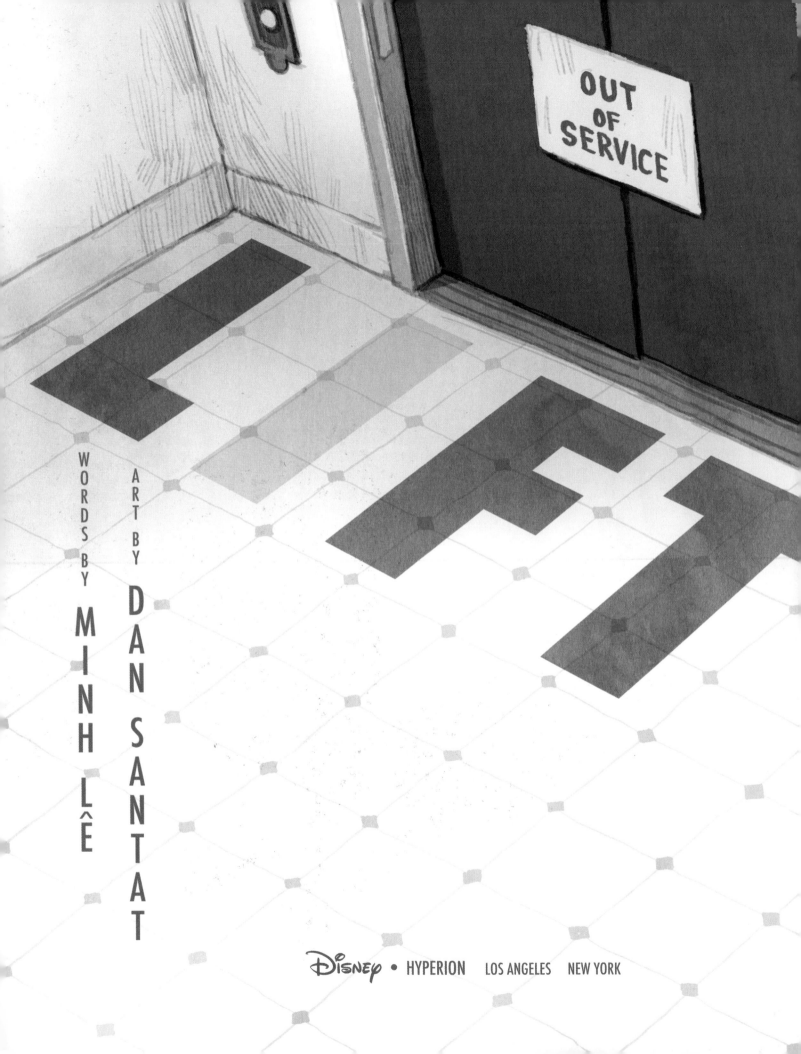

OUT
OF
SERVICE

LIFT

WORDS BY **MINH LÊ**

ART BY **DAN SANTAT**

Disney • HYPERION   LOS ANGELES   NEW YORK

Hi, my name is Iris.

When I'm feeling a bit down, there's one thing that always cheers me up:

PUSHING ELEVATOR BUTTONS.

Luckily, that's my job. Up or down, our floor or the lobby,

I always get to push the button.

Until one day...

Enough is enough. I know it's wrong, but I can't help myself. I push . . .

DING.

TAP
TAP
TAP

DING.

DING.

When we get back home, I just want to be alone.

I wish I could be anywhere but here.

DING!

Hang on—first dinner and then...

OUT OF THIS WORLD

I brought games!

CLICK

FINALLY.

CLICK

DING!

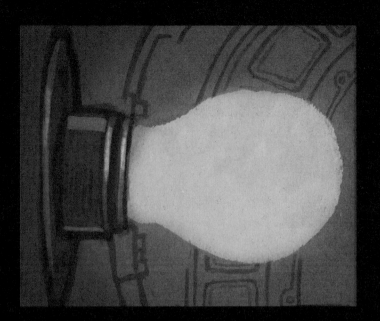

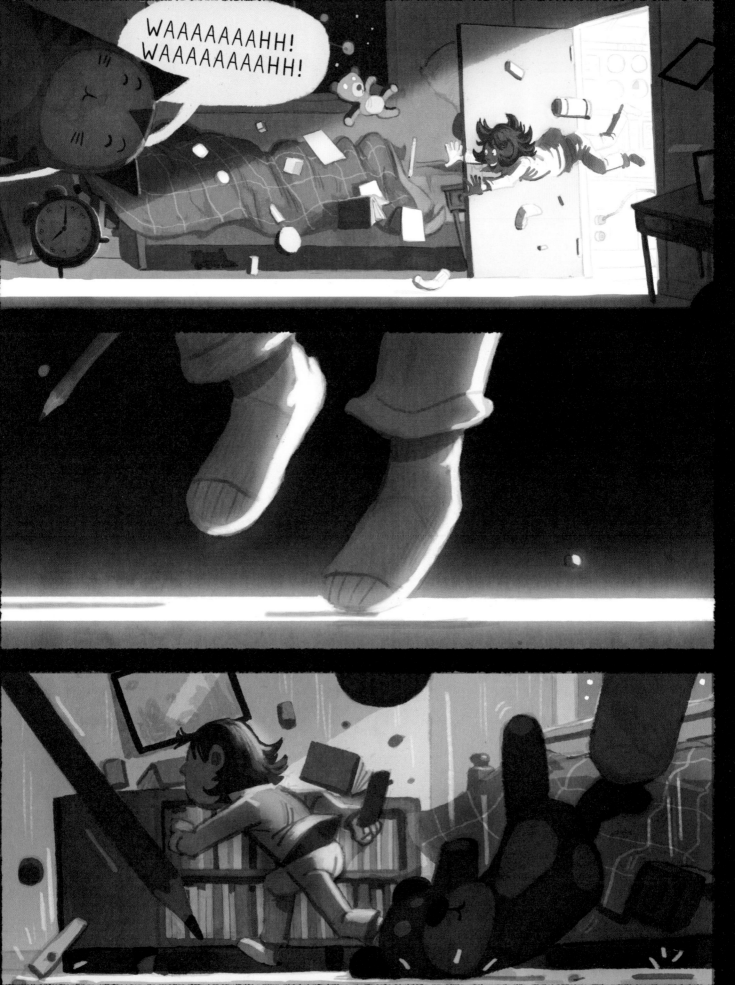

I know exactly
what you want...

SUMMIT

SUMMIT

YAWN

In the morning I wake up excited for my next visit,

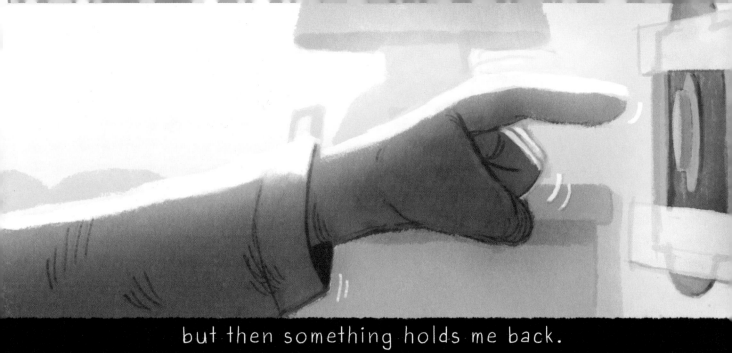

but then something holds me back.

After all, everyone can use a lift sometimes.

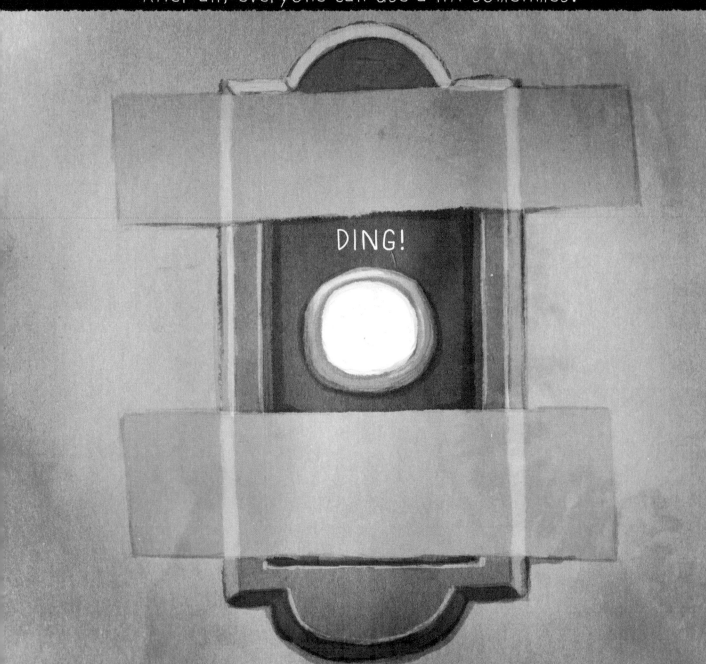

DING!

For my sisters, Tiên and Vi: Thank you for
a lifetime of lifting one another up. —M.L.

For Alek and Kyle. —D.S.

First Edition, May 2020 • 10 9 8 7 6 5 4 3 2 1
FAC-029191-20038 • Printed in Malaysia • This book is set in Danvetica
Library of Congress Control Number: 2019945115
ISBN 978-1-368-03692-4
Reinforced binding
Visit www.DisneyBooks.com